THE LION
First Book *of*
Nursery Stories

Text by Lois Rock
Illustrations copyright © 2013 Barbara Vagnozzi
This edition copyright © 2013 Lion Hudson

The right of Barbara Vagnozzi to be identified as the illustrator of this work has been asserted
by her in accordance with the Copyright, Designs and Patents Act 1988.

Published by Lion Children's Books
an imprint of
Lion Hudson plc
Wilkinson House, Jordan Hill Road,
Oxford OX2 8DR, England
www.lionhudson.com/lionchildrens

ISBN 978 0 7459 6341 9

First edition 2013

A catalogue record for this book is available
from the British Library

Printed and bound in China, February 2013, LH23

THE LION
First Book *of*
Nursery Stories

RETOLD BY LOIS ROCK
ILLUSTRATED BY BARBARA VAGNOZZI

LION
CHILDREN'S

Contents

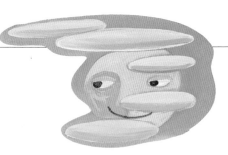

The Three Wishes

A story from England

There was once a woodcutter who lived in a great, dark forest.

The work was always slow, and often dreary.

Those who bought the timber always haggled over the price they would pay.

The poor woodcutter never had much money to bring home to his wife.

"Perhaps today will bring you better luck." That's what his wife always said as she handed him a satchel of bread and cheese, and sometimes an apple.

Usually the woodcutter sighed and simply said, "Perhaps."

One day he smiled. "Yesterday evening I found a magnificent old oak tree," he said. "I will be able to sell oak wood for good money."

The woodcutter tramped along many winding paths to reach the oak.
  He lifted his axe high so that he could give a really good…

"STOP!"

The shrill cry made the woodcutter tumble over backwards and into some raspberry bushes.
  "Please don't cut my tree," said the voice.

The woodcutter looked around to see who might be speaking, but all he saw was a tiny shadow slipping into a hollow by the oak tree's roots.

The woodcutter had heard many tales of the little folk and was rather afraid.

"I'll leave your tree alone and be on my way," he said.

For a moment there was silence. Then the little voice spoke again.

"Thank you very kindly. In return, I shall grant you three wishes."

The woodcutter scrambled to his feet and hurried off. Somehow he took a wrong path, and it took most of the day to find his way back to his wife and cottage, having cut no wood at all.

"You're early," said his wife. "The bean stew has barely begun to boil."

"Bean stew again!" said the man. "I wish I could have a nice big sausage instead."

ddd ding!

All at once, down the chimney came a huge sausage that smelled delicious.

His wife shrieked in dismay.

"Aargh! Help!"

"Let me explain," said her husband; and he told her all about the mysterious voice and the promise of three wishes.

When at last the poor woman understood, she was angry.

"Three wishes and you've just gone and used one for a

sausage!" she exclaimed. "It's money we need, not sausages. I wish that sausage would go and fasten itself to the end of your nose."

ddddding!

At once the sausage flew onto the end of the man's nose and stuck there.

"Oh no! Oh dear!"

Try as they might, neither of them could get the sausage to come unstuck.

"I just wish it would come off!" cried the man.

At once the sausage fell off.

The man and his wife stared at each other with relief. "Well, I won't miss what I never had," said the wife.

And as they both agreed, the sausage tasted excellent with the bean stew.

The Greedy Monkey

A story from Pakistan

When the forest trees were in fruit, there was so much to
eat! Little Monkey chose only the best: yellow-green guavas
that promised pink juiciness inside; sweet purple figs; golden,
gorgeous persimmons; amber mangoes; and ruby-red
pomegranates with seeds that glistened in the sunlight. Mmm.

  Of course, Little Monkey wasn't the only creature who
liked these feasts of the forest. As the season went by, the fruit
became harder to find. Little Monkey could no longer be so
fussy about which to choose: he had to learn to like the fruits
that were a little squashy and others that were just a bit too
hard and, ooh, quite sour.

The time came when Little Monkey couldn't find any more fruit. He was getting hungry.

As he clambered among the tree tops, he smelled something.

sniff sniff

Yes, very definitely there was a smell of…

sniff sniff

nuts.

Walnuts, he guessed. But there weren't any walnut trees nearby. That could only mean one thing.

Some other creature had picked quite a lot of nuts and hidden them in a secret store.

But carefully looking and…

sniff sniff

sniffing, Little Monkey was determined to find that store.

There it was!

A hole in a tree – quite a small hole – with an unmistakable smell of walnuts.

Little Monkey held his fingers straight as he dipped his hand inside.

Ooh yes. He felt all around. There were lots of nuts. He opened his hand and curled his fingers around them to take the biggest fistful possible.

He opened his mouth wide so he could stuff it full of walnuts, and pulled.

And pulled.

Oh dear. His fist was too big.

Nearby a hornbill cackled. Little Monkey

heard a
flapping of wings.
The hornbill perched on a
nearby branch and poked Little
Monkey with his beak.

"You can't take so many," it said.
"Don't be so greedy."

"I'll have as many as I can grab," said
the Little Monkey. He squeezed the fistful
tight and pulled again.

"It doesn't pay to be greedy, Little
Monkey," cackled the hornbill.

Little Monkey would not give up. He pulled. He tugged. He screwed up his face really hard and pulled again. The hornbill lost interest and flapped away.

Little Monkey tried again. Really, his fist would not come out.

Oh panic! He was stuck!

With a yowl, Little Monkey let all the nuts go and pulled his unclenched fist away.

"I don't even like nuts," he said, as he swung off.

For a little while the forest was quiet. Then came a rustling and a scrabbling. Two squirrels came scampering along the branches to the hole.

One reached a paw inside.

"Here's one for you," it said to its friend. It reached in again. "And one for me."

They sat and munched, listening to the cackle of a hornbill.

cackle cackle

The Bell of Atri

A story from Italy

Sometimes it seems that the people who talk the loudest get their own way. Those who are shy get pushed aside. It isn't very fair.

"It isn't fair at all," declared King John of Atri.

"I am going to have a tower built in the main square. From it I will hang a silver bell with a rope that reaches right down to the ground.

"Anyone who thinks they have been treated wrongly can go and ring that bell. It will summon my wisest judges to the square. They will listen to the complaint and right any wrong."

At first it was still the people with the loudest voices who dared set the silver bell swinging.

They got the justice they demanded.

Soon the shyer people grew bold enough to go and pull the rope. They too got the justice they so deserved.

As the years went by, young and old understood that the king wanted everyone to be treated fairly. Those who worked hard could get proper pay.

Those who had fallen on hard times could get help.

Those who were eager to learn could find a trade.

And it got better. Anyone who was tempted to do wrong had to think about what might happen. The jingle of ill-gotten money was nothing compared to the CLANG of the bell.

The bell was used less and less often. No one noticed when the rope began to fray, not even when the fibres were so worn away that children could no longer reach it.

Then one day a herald arrived in the marketplace to say that the king was coming on a visit. Within minutes.

"There's no time to get a new rope," they exclaimed. "Whatever can we do?"

"Oh… I have a bundle of hay," said a farmers boy. "I can braid it into a rope that will last long enough."

And so the fix was made.

A few days later, when everyone was idling in the warm afternoon sun, the silver bell rang out.

Kerlang, kerlang, kerlang!

Everyone rushed to see who was in such trouble.

It was a horse, skinny and bony, munching on the hay.

Of course, the judges came rushing into the square at once, and so did the king.

"Whose horse is this?" asked the king. "How dare they treat their horse so unkindly?"

"I know," said a boy. "It belongs to the old soldier who lives on the hill.

"He tells stories about how the horse carried him into battle, and how brave they both were."

The king and the judges sent for the man. He came in a fine woollen cloak and good leather boots and everyone could see that he was not poor.

Indeed, when the judges asked for his side of the story, the old soldier confessed that he was comfortably off.

"Then your horse must be comfortable too," the judges declared. "You must give him pasture and shelter, and extra oats in the winter."

"There is one more thing," added the king. "You must pay for a new rope for the bell.

"For everyone deserves to be treated fairly – even the animals."

The Miller and His Donkey

A story by Aesop, from Ancient Greece

The miller was on his way to market and he was feeling very cheerful.

"We're sure to be able to sell our little donkey," he told his son. "Then we'll be able to do as we please with the money."

The three had not got very far before they heard laughing. Some women by a village well clearly thought something hilarious.

"Can you believe it? They've got a donkey and they're plodding along next to it!"

"I wonder if they have a cart they pull along the road to spare their ox?"

"Do you think they bark so their dog can go on sleeping?"

Suddenly the miller felt rather foolish. "Come on, boy, you ride," he said.

Some distance further along, the three passed a group of old men who were sitting under a tree watching the world go by.

"Young people today!" the miller heard one saying. "They're so idle, think only of themselves."

"You young rascal," called another to the miller's son. "Show some respect. Let your father ride. He's got more reason to be weary."

"Sorry, Dad," said the boy. "I don't want people thinking bad things about me."

The donkey carried the miller and plodded along at a steady pace.

The son trailed along, sometimes stopping to listen to the birds or to watch lizards sunning themselves on stones.

Later, as he ran to catch up with his father, they reached a village where women were watching their children play.

"You mean old dad," said one of the women. "That little lad can hardly keep up and you didn't even notice."

"Oh, sorry son," said the father. "Here, come and sit behind me. It's not far to go now anyway."

As the two rode along, a man from the town came out along the road.

He stopped in amazement.

"Is that your donkey?" asked the townsman.

"It is," replied the miller.

"I can't believe you'd be so cruel to your own poor beast," said the townsman. "It's so little. Your legs are nearly trailing on the ground.

"You two could carry the donkey more easily than it can carry you."

The miller and his son got off at once.

"That's a good point," said the miller. "Come on, lad. Let's see if we can carry our donkey."

They found a long branch and tied the donkey to it by its legs.

The donkey did not like being tied in that way, nor did it like being carried upside down.

It began braying and making a dreadful racket.

People on their way to market turned to see the miller and his son carrying a donkey over the bridge.

The donkey thrashed and kicked itself free.

With a splash it fell into the river and was swept away.

"Oh dear," said the miller. "Oh dear, oh dear, oh dear.

"I tried to please everyone and ended up pleasing no one.

"Now we've lost the donkey and the money I was hoping to make from it."

Sorrowfully he and his son trudged home.

The Three Little Pigs

A story from England

Mother Pig had an announcement for her three little pigs. Well, not so little anymore. That was the point.

"I've taken care of you for a long time," she said. "I've done my best. The time has come for you to leave home and seek your fortune."

The three little pigs squealed. The squeals were partly excitement:

"Yippee!"

And partly fear.

"Yikes."

Because Mother Pig was being entirely serious.

The very next day the three little pigs took their few possessions and started out, each going their separate way.

The first little pig met a farmer with a cartload of straw. Well, it had been a cartload of straw, but it had just fallen off the back of the cart. Now the farmer was mumbling at it very angrily.

The little pig had an idea.

"I could take care of that straw for you," he said.

It was agreed in no time.

The little pig used the straw to build a house. It looked like a haystack but it was, in fact, a house.

The little pig sat inside enjoying his easy success. "From pigsty to palace," he said.

Just then, there came a knock at the door.

"Little pig, little pig, let me come in."

The little pig ran to the window. What he saw was not as he feared: it was much, much worse.

The big bad wolf was outside, and it gave the little pig a wicked wink.

"Not by the hair on my chinny chin chin," exclaimed the little pig.

The wolf smirked.

"Then I'll huff and I'll puff and I'll BLOW your house in."

The wolf huffed. The wolf puffed, and his bad breath buffeted the straw house until it blew to bits.

Then the big bad wolf gobbled up the first little pig.

The second little pig had started out into the woods. There he met a woodcutter who was making a bonfire of unwanted branches.

The second little pig had a flash of inspiration.

"Oh, Mr Woodcutter. Could you let me take those sticks, please?"

It was agreed in no time. In a corner of the forest, the second little pig made a ring of good poles and wove twigs between them. Then he put a tall pole in the middle to support a leafy roof.

"A stick house is sturdy," he congratulated himself.

Just then, there came a knock at the door.

"Little pig, little pig, let me come in."

The second little pig ran to the window. What he saw was not as he feared. It was much, much worse.

The big bad wolf was outside, and it gave the little pig a wicked wink.

"Not by the hair on my chinny chin chin," exclaimed the second little pig.

The wolf snarled.

"Then I'll huff and I'll puff and I'll BLOW your house in."

The wolf huffed. The wolf puffed. Then he puffed and he huffed until he had puffed just enough to shake that stick house to bits.

Then, with a snarl, the big bad wolf gobbled up the second little pig.

The third little pig walked along the river bank. There she met a man who was stacking up some bricks and grumbling to himself.

"So the man orders a load of bricks and then changes his house design," said the brick maker. "All these are going to go to waste."

"Oh," said the third little pig, "I could make good use of them."

It was agreed in no time. However, building a brick house took a very long time. The bricks were heavy. There were delays with the weather. The design – with a splendid kitchen range – ran into all kinds of snags. The third little pig almost changed the whole plan for it part way through.

But in the end it was done.

"A brick house is brilliant," she said. "And the fireplace will be splendid for cooking over."

Just then, there came a knock at the door.

"Little pig, little pig, let me come in."

The third little pig ran to the window. It was just as she had expected: another problem to solve.

The big bad wolf was outside, and it gave the little pig a wicked wink.

"Not by the hair on my chinny chin chin," exclaimed the third little pig.

The wolf smiled.

"Then I'll huff and I'll puff and I'll BLOW your house in."

The wolf **huffed**.

The wolf **puffed**.

Then he **puffed** and he **huffed**.

Then he **huffed** and he **puffed**.

Then he had a sit down and a bit of a think.

He spoke simperingly. "It's a wonderful house," he said. "Might I come in and have a look around?"

For an answer, the third little pig simply slid another bolt across the door on the inside.

"Would you come and advise me on how to improve my lair?" said the wolf. "I'll pay, of course."

For an answer, the third little pig drew the curtains.

The sun set. Twilight came. The wolf slipped through the shadows and climbed onto the roof.

He climbed onto the chimney.

"Here I come," he howled.

Meanwhile the third little pig had lit the fire and was boiling a big pot of water. The wolf fell into the boiling water and yowled.

Not for long. The little pig popped the lid on the pan and made a stew.

"Delicious," she said, as she wolfed it down.

The Emperor's New Clothes

A story by Hans Christian Andersen, from Denmark

The emperor struck a pose in front of the full-length mirror. His tailor whisked away the cloth so his reflection would be revealed.

"Voila!"

The emperor was clearly disappointed.

"Very nice," he said flatly. "You've got the traditional look down to a fine art.

"But where's the WOW?"

Happily for the tailor, the chamberlain tiptoed in.

"Your Majesty," he whispered. "Outside are two men from a foreign fashion house. They say that it would be their dream to make the robes for your next royal parade. They claim they are able to weave cloth the like of which the world has never seen."

"Oh, very interesting," said the emperor.

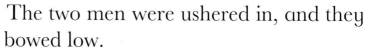

The two men were ushered in, and they bowed low.

"Your Majesty," they said. "We are delighted to offer you a world first: fabric so light and fine that it is appreciated only by those with the very best taste.

"Indeed, it is so fine that some say it is invisible! How they let themselves down by their words. They show themselves to be fools.

"We have heard of your judgment as a leader of people and a leader of good taste. Might we make robes for you?"

"Oh, I would love that!" said the emperor. "Show me some clothing designs at once!"

"Ah!" said the men. "For you, everything must be original. If you provide us with your choice of gold cord and silk thread, we will create a masterpiece just for you."

The emperor clapped his hands.

"Chamberlain," he said. "Give these men all they need."

To the tailor he added, "Let them have your workshop, won't you?"

The two weavers kept the workshop locked when they were working and double-locked when they were out. The emperor was impatient for the styling and fitting to take place. He sent his chamberlain to check if the fabric was ready.

When the chamberlain was allowed in to see the samples, he gasped.

He couldn't see any cloth at all. Was he one of those fools who lacked the intelligence, the taste, the wisdom? If he let that be known, he would lose his job.

So he blustered. "It's all exquisite. Wonderful."

"We're delighted ourselves," said one of the weavers; "but now we've chosen an even more extravagant design for the outfit. Could you supply more gold cord and silk thread to make extra fabric, please?"

The emperor happily agreed to their request.

He was very excited when he was invited to his first fitting. But oh dear. He couldn't see the robes they draped around him.

Was he a fool? He would lose the respect of everyone, including his chamberlain.

So he blustered.

"These… are… superb. Oh wow. Wow! Triple wow."

Behind him the men were whispering.

"We were just thinking," they said, "that we should make special undergarments in the same fabric, to avoid their unsightly lines showing."

"Oh… I don't know," said the emperor, feeling rather alarmed.

The men shook their heads. "You don't want to skimp now," they said. "Not having invested this much."

So, on the day of the parade, the king was attired completely in the wonderful cloth.

"Ooh," he said. He was feeling rather cold.

"Aaah," said the chamberlain.

"I've never seen such a suit," said his tailor, just a hint of anxiety in his voice.

"Your people are waiting for you," said the weavers. "It has been a privilege to work for you. We have been enriched by the time spent in your household."

A fanfare sounded.

The chief herald cried aloud:

"The emperor! Show yourselves worthy to be his subjects."

The crowd had been told about the wonderful clothes. They cheered. They roared. Many tailors had notebooks so they could copy the designs… but they were too awestruck to do anything.

Except for one little boy. He gazed, open-mouthed.

"The emperor!" he said.

'He's got no clothes on!"

Stone Soup

A story from Portugal

It was late afternoon, and market day was over. In the village square the stallholders were packing away the last of their produce and saying goodbye.

Then a poor man, wearing the cockleshell of a pilgrim, came along the road.

He sat on the edge of the well and kicked off his dusty boots.

"Is there a place I could stay?" he enquired.

People shook their heads. "It doesn't look as if he could pay for a room, does it?" whispered one woman to a friend.

"I haven't got enough to spare to offer lodging for free!" agreed her companion.

It was the poorest person in the village – an elderly widow – who invited the pilgrim to stay.

She took him to her tiny cottage and roused the fire.

"I've only got a little bread," she apologized.

The pilgrim shrugged. "I have an old recipe for making soup from almost nothing," he said. "I shall just go and get all I need."

He put a pot of water over the fire to boil, and then went out into the garden. He returned with a smooth, round stone that he wiped clean. Carefully he slipped it into the pot.

As the steam began to rise, he dipped in a spoon and tasted the liquid.

"Mm," he said. "Not bad. Did I see some herbs growing in your garden?"

"Ooh, yes," said the woman. "Rosemary and thyme. I'll go and get some."

The children who lived next door followed the old woman back to her house, curious to see more of the pilgrim with his battered clothes and tattered pack.

"What's in the pot?" they asked.

"Stone soup," replied the pilgrim. "Now with lovely herbs. It's better with onion, too, but we have none."

"We've got a string of them," said the children. "We'll get some."

They returned with two onions. They also brought some newly pulled carrots.

"We usually have carrots in soup," they explained.

"Oh, this is turning into the best soup," said the pilgrim as he added the vegetables.

The children went and whispered to their friends. Once the news was out, other children began arriving with other ingredients: a few cloves of garlic, a huge pumpkin, and handful of sunflower seeds, a little jar of salt.

The pilgrim added everything very carefully, tasting all the while.

It seemed that every child in the village must have brought something when he stood up. "Perfect," he said.

"Everyone will want some of this."

And they did. The simple soup had become a feast.

The Three Billy Goats Gruff

A folktale from Norway

The littlest billy goat had never thought much about the meadow on the other side of the bridge.

But now that he and his brothers had eaten all the grass on their side, he could think of almost nothing else: the lush grass, the bright flowers, the tender green saplings.

"Yum!"

Except for one thing: the troll. His mother had told him about a troll who lived under the bridge – a greedy monster who ATE whoever dared cross the bridge.

Then again, it was a story. No one had ever seen the troll. Slowly, slowly, ever so quietly, the littlest billy goat tiptoed onto the bridge.

He was just over half way when he heard a

ROAR.

"Who's crossing MY bridge?" growled the troll. He was huge and hairy and he had ENORMOUS teeth.

"I'll have you for supper."

"Oh, don't eat me," pleaded the littlest billy goat. "I'm hardly a snack for you. You'd want a bigger meal – and my older brother is coming behind me."

As the troll turned to look, the littlest billy goat skipped over the bridge and into the meadow.

The second billy goat had been too busy trying to reach the higher leaves on a tree to notice what had happened. When he turned to find his kid brother, he saw that he was grazing happily in the meadow on the other side of the bridge.

"Oh, so it is safe to cross," he said to himself. And off he went.

He was just over half way when he heard a ROAR.

"Who's crossing MY bridge?" growled the troll. He was huge and hairy and he had ENORMOUS teeth.

"Ooh yes: the older brother will make a delicious supper."

"Oh, don't eat me," pleaded the second billy goat. "I've been eating wild garlic and you won't like the taste of me. Anyway, my older brother is coming behind me and he's much bigger."

As the troll turned to look, the second billy goat skipped over the bridge and into the meadow.

The third billy goat had actually been eating the last patch of clover. It was greedy of him, but then he was the oldest and the biggest of his brothers. He was astonished to see them happily munching in the meadow on the other side of the bridge.

He galloped to join them, and his hooves were clattering on the bridge when...

"RRAAAGH!"

"Who's crossing MY bridge?" growled the troll. He was huge and hairy and he had ENORMOUS teeth. "I'm hungry for my supper!" roared the troll. He climbed onto the bridge and reached out his warty hands. The third billy goat stepped further and further back until he was almost back in the first meadow. The troll was in the middle of the bridge, preparing to pounce, when…

SPLASH

The biggest billy goat
butted that old troll off the bridge and
into the river.

He was swept away and no one ever heard of him
again.

The three billy goats were able to cross the bridge in
safety whenever they wanted and there was always
plenty for them to eat.

The Ugly Duckling

Based on a story by Hans Christian Andersen, from Denmark

"Why do you have to be so
CLUMSY?"
Those were the first words the
duckling could remember his mother
saying; and really, he knew she
loved him.

"Don't put your big
FEET on me!"

That was what his brothers and
sisters always complained about.
"You're so BIG."
"And so HEAVY."

When the little family went out and about in the farmyard, it was the ugly duckling who got all the unkindness.

"You're a hefty one – do you want a fight?" challenged the cockerel, pecking at him.

"You're not very nimble, are you?" teased the cat. "I could easily POUNCE on you."

"You're the greediest old duckling I've ever seen," said the girl who came scattering feed. "SHOO, will you, and let your sweet little brothers and sisters get something to eat."

"Oh, do get lost!" agreed one of the clucking sisters.

So the ugly duckling did get himself lost – as far away as he could get. "I just didn't fit in with my family," he said to himself, "and I was a disappointment to my mother." The thought made him shed a tear.

He settled himself down in a wide marsh. "I'll just be… a wild duck," he said.

Just then, two wild ducks flew up. "Oh. Aren't you odd? You're not one of us," said one.

"You're a migrant, aren't you?" said the other. "Well, keep to your own patch of marsh, will you? Don't think you can come helping yourself in ours."

After that, some young geese came by. "What a funny shape your beak is," they said. "And your feathers: you look as if you haven't preened yourself properly."

The goose mother came hurrying to find her offspring. "Now hurry away with me," she said. "The hunters will soon be out and about and we must fly."

She spoke sharply to the ugly duckling: "Don't think you can tag along. Stick with your own kind, if you don't mind."

The ugly duckling was left alone and miserable. He got by, eating slugs and worms and such, but he had no friends.

One day he saw a flock of huge white birds flying overhead and far away, and deep inside he longed to go with them.

Winter came. Food was hard to find. The day came when the pond froze over and the snow fell in big flakes.

The days were icy; the nights were frosty. The ugly duckling wished more and more that he had never hatched. When he went to sleep, he wished he would not wake up.

One morning, the sun shone warm and gold. Small birds sang around him. He noticed green shoots among the reeds.

Before he knew it, spring had come, and with it the flock of great white birds he had seen leaving before winter set in.

As he stood up for a closer look, the swans came rushing and flapping to greet him.

"My, aren't you brave and strong to have stayed here," said one.

"And how handsome you are," said another.

The ugly duckling hung his head. Was this some new kind of teasing?

"Don't you believe us? Go out onto the clear water and look," said the swans. "You're a swan."

So he went and he looked and he lifted his snowy-white neck.
"I'm a swan," he said in amazement. "How proud I am to be
just what I am."

Go Fast Slowly

A story from the Philippines

The farmer had gone early to his melon patch,
to cut the fruit he would take to market.

"What a wonderful crop," he exclaimed. "The
fruits are round and ripe and there's not a mark
on them. I can look forward to getting an excellent
price for each of them."

The more he looked under the big green leaves, the
more melons the farmer found.

The more melons he found, the more he had to pick.

The more he picked, the more he had to load into his cart.

"Oh dear, oh dear: I'm later than I should be for setting off,"
he said. "Now I shall have to hurry."

As he drove his donkey cart along, he had an idea. "There's
a track that people from the next village along use," he said
to himself. "They've always said it's a useful short cut.
Today is the day to try."

The track began well enough; but the farmer had not gone far before it began to get bumpier. "Oh dear," he said. "I hope I haven't made a mistake in choosing this way."

Then he saw a group of children from the village, picking berries from the side of the track.

"Hello!" he called. "Do you know how long it will take me to reach the town this way?"

The eldest girl looked up.

"It depends," she said. "If you go slowly, you can be there in ten minutes. If you go fast, it will take at least half an hour."

The farmer waved his thanks, but as he drove on he shook his head. "The poor girl got all muddled," he said. "What she should have said was that if I hurry, I can be in town in ten minutes."

And with that, he shook the reins to make the donkey go fast.

The cart rumbled along until…

CLONK

One of the wheels hit
a bump
   and that made the
cart jolt

and that made the melons come tumbling forward
   and the rolling melons so scared the donkey that it gave a big kick.

The big kick knocked the cart right over.

"Oh dear and oh disaster!" cried the farmer. "Now the melons will be bruised and it will take ages to pick them up."

He began to gather them, one by one, and pack them into his cart. He had almost finished the job when the children came along.

They had almost filled their berry baskets and were carrying them ever so carefully so as not to spill the fruit.

"Oh dear," said the eldest girl, as she and her friends helped lift the last melons onto the cart. "You must have gone very fast. You've been on the track nearly an hour."

The Boy Who Cried Wolf

A story by Aesop, from Ancient Greece

The shepherd boy pulled his cloak close around him. The night was getting cold.

He thought about soup. Not that he had any soup out there on the hillside. Oh no. Soup was what he would have been having if he'd been at home.

All he had was bread and cheese. In fact, it was time to eat the bread and cheese.

munch munch munch

Suddenly he stopped munching. Could he hear something? Something creeping through the undergrowth? Something with bright eyes glinting in the moonlight?
Could it be a…

"Wolf," he cried. "Wolf! Wolf!"

The people outside the tavern heard.
"Quick!" they cried. "We must go and save our sheep."
They rushed up the hill brandishing sticks and pitchforks and… beer tankards.
"Where?" they cried. "Where's the wolf?"

The shepherd boy bit his lip.

"It's gone," he said. "I was sure it was there, by the sheepfold, but it went as soon as I shouted."

"Oh well," said the villagers. "Never mind."

They all trooped off to the village, leaving the shepherd boy alone again.

One by one the village lights went out. A wind sprang up. A cloud drifted in front of the moon.

The boy strained to see. Was that a rabbit in the bushes?

Or a robber: Or was it a…

"Wolf!" he shrieked. "Wolf!"

The lights went on in the village. The men swarmed up the hillside, brandishing sticks and pitchforks and… fireside pokers.

"Where?" they shouted. "We'll get him."

The cloud drifted away from the moon. The boy dropped his head.

"It's gone," he said. "It was there in the shadows but… not any more."

The villagers grumbled a bit as they ambled off down the hill.

The shepherd boy's uncle came and patted him on the shoulder.

"Now, you've got to stay alert, young man, but don't panic at nothing."

The boy nodded.

The villagers reached their homes and dimmed the lights. An owl hooted and another answered. There was a bark. A fox? A deer?

"Maa," cried a lamb in a high, babyish bleat, and the mother lambs all baaed low, comforting noises.

The shepherd boy giggled.

"Wolf," he said in a high, babyish voice. Nothing happened.

"Wolf," he called again, only louder.

Then he shrieked, "Wolf!"

That set the sheep off good and proper. They baaed and they jostled and that made the shepherd boy panic.

"Wolf!" he cried again.

A shout rang out from the village. "We're coming, lad!" shouted his uncle.

The villagers came rushing up the hillside with sticks and pitchforks and even bed-warming pans.

They slowed to a walk as they reached the shepherd boy.

"Where's the wolf?" asked the shepherd boy's uncle.

The boy shrugged. "I… thought the sheep had smelled one," he said.

"Oh," said his uncle.

"Right," said the villagers. And they went back down the hill to their beds.

The shepherd boy sat glumly. He felt in his bag for the last few crumbs of bread. He wished there'd been cake as well. He reached for his pipe and played a little tune.

Then he took off his hat, laid it upside down on the ground, and tried to throw stones into it.

He was doing really rather well when he saw some shapes flitting through the wood. He froze in fear. They were coming this way.

Suddenly a whole pack of wolves came out of the shadows and approached the sheepfold, snarling softly.

"Wolf!" screamed the boy.

"Wolf! Wolf!"

Down in the village, everyone heard. They turned over in their beds.

Even the boy's uncle groaned. "He'll learn in the end," he sighed, as he buried his head under the pillow.

In the morning, all they found was the shepherd boy's hat.

Walnuts and Pumpkins

A story from Turkey

The wise man was lazing in the warm evening sun. A tall old walnut tree cast a pleasant shade.

Of course, a wise man is given to deep thoughts, and he took the opportunity to reflect on the wisdom of the world's great Maker.

"Such a lovely tree the Maker has created," he said to himself, "and so many delicious nuts dangling from the boughs. They are a treat from harvest time all through the hungry winter months."

He sat up to look around.

"The pumpkins are ripening nicely," he said to himself. "They too will provide through the winter. How generous is the world's great Maker."

He pondered some more. "It's odd, though, isn't it," he thought, "to create such a mighty tree for such tiny walnuts, while the giant pumpkins grow on a spindly vine?"

Thinking this, he dozed off.

A walnut fell from the tree and hit him on the nose.

He woke up and rubbed the sore spot.

"Oh dear," he exclaimed. Then he paused for a moment's reflection. "If pumpkins grew on that tree," he declared to himself, "I would have been badly hurt. How wise is the world's great Maker."

The Man Who Never Lied

A story from Africa

Down in the marketplace, the men roared with laughter.

"You made up that story," they said to the one who had been speaking. "Fibber," they added. Then they all laughed again.

"No I didn't," came the reply. "Twenty days' journey from here there is a wise man who has never told a lie – neither a whopper nor a white lie; never a falsehood nor a fib."

While the men were joking and teasing one another, it so happened that the king rode by.

He asked to know what was so amusing. When he found out, he was curious to know more.

He spoke to a servant. "I'd like to meet that wise man. Go and get him for me."

The wise man was shabbily dressed. But he seemed not in the least daunted to be brought before the king.

"Is it true," asked the king, "that you have never told a lie?"

"It is," said the wise man.

"Is it your resolve never to lie?"

"It is," said the wise man.

The king looked impressed. "A worthy aim," he said; "but take care. The lie is cunning. It seeks to make its home on every tongue."

A week went by. Early in the morning, the king summoned the wise man a second time.

He arrived just as the king was about to go hunting. Indeed, the king had grasped his horse by the mane and put his left foot in the stirrup ready to mount.

"Go to my summer palace," said the king. "The queen is there. Tell her we will be there for a feast at noon tomorrow."

The wise man bowed and went.

"Now we shall have some fun," said the king to his retinue. "We shan't go hunting; instead we will have some music.

"Tomorrow we will go and remind that wise man how easy it is to be made a fool of."

Meanwhile, the wise man hurried to the palace and explained why he had come.

"Maybe you should prepare a feast, and maybe not," he said. "Maybe the king will come by noon, but maybe he will not."

"I want a clear answer," said the queen. "Will the king come, or not?"

"I cannot say," said the wise man. "I do not know what he did after I left. Did he swing up onto his horse, or did he take his left foot from the stirrup?

"Did he go hunting, or did he change his plans?

"Will he arrive as planned, or will something happen to make that impossible?"

The next day, the king arrived, but only as twilight was falling. As he approached, he saw servants uncovering the feast they had put on the table.

The king smiled. "The wise man who told you to go to all this trouble misled you," he said. "I'm afraid he did not tell the truth."

But the queen told her husband exactly what the wise man had said, and that they had been prepared for him to arrive at any time or not at all.

Then the king knew: a wise man only declares to be true the things he has seen with his own eyes.

The Gingerbread Man

A story from Europe

The little old woman smiled.

"One of these is just perfect," she said, as she lifted a tray from the oven. "Now I can make the finest little gingerbread man."

The gingerbread man cooled, and she mixed up some icing. Then she used the icing to draw a face and clothes on him. She added two currants for eyes and three dried cherries for his buttons.

Her husband came in from working in the fields.
"What a treat!" he said.
But at that, the gingerbread man jumped up and ran along to the open window.

"You can't catch me – I'm the gingerbread man!" he cried.

He jumped out of the window and began running down the road.
The little old man and the little old woman ran after him.

Their young grandson was coming back from fishing. He saw the little old man and the little old woman running after the gingerbread man, and he began to run too.

The gingerbread man squealed with glee.

"Run, run, as fast as you can.
You can't catch me
I'm the gingerbread man,"

he cried.

A cow heard the commotion and she began to run: after the boy and the little old man and the little old woman, and all of them after the same thing.

"Run, run, as fast as you can.
You can't catch me
I'm the gingerbread man,"

laughed the gingerbread man.

After the cow came a donkey.

heehaw

After the donkey came a horse.

ne-eh-eh

After the horse came a bear.

grrowl

They clattered and galloped down the road, while far ahead they could hear a cry:

"Run, run, as fast as you can.
You can't catch me
I'm the gingerbread man."

But then the gingerbread man reached a river.

Oh no! He couldn't swim. If he dived and dunked, he would drown.

Just then, a fox came out from behind the bushes.

The gingerbread man gasped in fear.

"Don't be afraid," said the fox, with a sly smile. "I can help you cross the river. Just sit on my head and I'll swim you to the other side."

"Oh, thanks," said the gingerbread man.

As the fox swam across, the gingerbread man looked back and laughed.

There on the bank were the little old man and the little old woman and their grandson and the cow and the donkey and the horse and the bear. He began to chant again.

"Run, run, as fast as you can.
You can't catch me
I – "

But at that moment the fox leaped ashore. He tossed his head and flicked the cookie into the air. He caught it in his mouth and crunched it up.

"Mmm – a gingerbread man," he said.

Goldilocks and the Three Bears

A story from Europe

For as long as the little girl could remember, she had always been adored.

"Such a pretty girl," her grandpa said.

"Such a sweet smile," her grandma said.

"Such lovely fair curls," said her mama.

"My little Goldilocks," said her papa.

Goldilocks was quite used to getting her own way.

So she didn't care a bit that she was not supposed to go alone into the woods.

One day, she started out. She walked ever such a long way: down sunlit glades, through dappled shade, on past towering trees.

Then, to her surprise, she reached a clearing. There was a cottage: quite small, and very neat and tidy.

She went to the door and knocked. There was no answer. She knocked again.

When there was still no answer, she turned the handle and opened the door into the kitchen.

Everything she saw came in three sizes.

Goldilocks went to the biggest chair at the table and took a spoonful of porridge from the biggest bowl.

"Ow! That's too hot," she said.

She went to the middle-sized chair and took a spoonful of porridge from the middle-sized bowl.

"Ew, that's too cold," she said.

She went to the little chair and took a spoonful of porridge from the little bowl.

"Mmm, that's just right," she said, and she ate it all up.

She went into the next room.

There were three fireside chairs.

She went and sat on the biggest chair. "This is too high," she complained.

She went and sat on the middle-sized chair. "This is too low," she grumbled.

She went and sat on the little chair. "This is just right," she said. But as she leaned back…

CRASH

The little chair broke into pieces.

"Oh dear," said Goldilocks. She picked herself up and went up the stairs.

There were three beds. Goldilocks jumped onto the biggest.

"Oh, that's too hard," she said.

She clambered onto the middle-sized bed. "Ooh, that one's too soft," she said.

She lay down on the little bed. "This one is lovely," she said, and fell fast asleep under the quilt.

Now, Goldilocks had not given a thought to who might actually live in the house. In fact, it belonged to three bears: Father Bear was the biggest, Mother Bear was middle size, and Baby Bear was just little.

Father Bear walked to the table.

"Someone has been eating my porridge," he growled in a deep voice.

Mother Bear walked to the table.

"Someone has been eating my porridge," she said in a scolding kind of voice.

"Someone has been eating my porridge and eaten it all up," squealed little Baby Bear.

The three bears went into the next room.

"Someone has been sitting on my chair," growled Father Bear in a deep voice.

"Someone has been sitting on my chair," said Mother Bear in a scolding kind of voice.

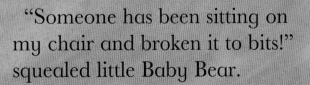

"Someone has been sitting on my chair and broken it to bits!" squealed little Baby Bear.

The three bears crept up the stairs.

"Someone has been sleeping in my bed," growled Father Bear in a deep voice.

"Someone has been sleeping in my bed," said Mother Bear in a scolding kind of voice.

"Someone has been sleeping in my bed," squealed little Baby Bear.

"AND SHE'S STILL HERE!"

At that, Goldilocks woke up. She saw the bears and she screamed. Then she ran down the stairs and out of the house and through the trees and all the way back into the sunshine and the path that led her home.

After that, she always did as she was told, and whenever she wanted something, she always said, "Please."